Pit Pat Pit Pat

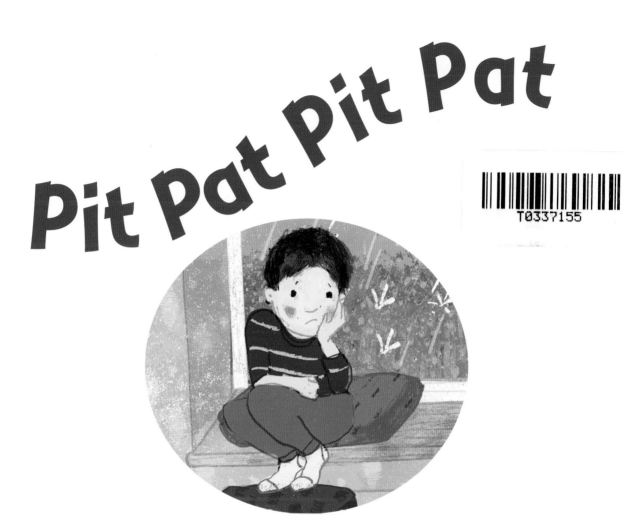

Written by Pranika Sharma

Illustrated by Sally Garland

Collins

pit pat pit pat

nap nap nap

Tim sits.

Dad naps.

nap nap

pit pat pit pat

Tim pads.

pit pat

Tim taps Dad.

Dad naps.

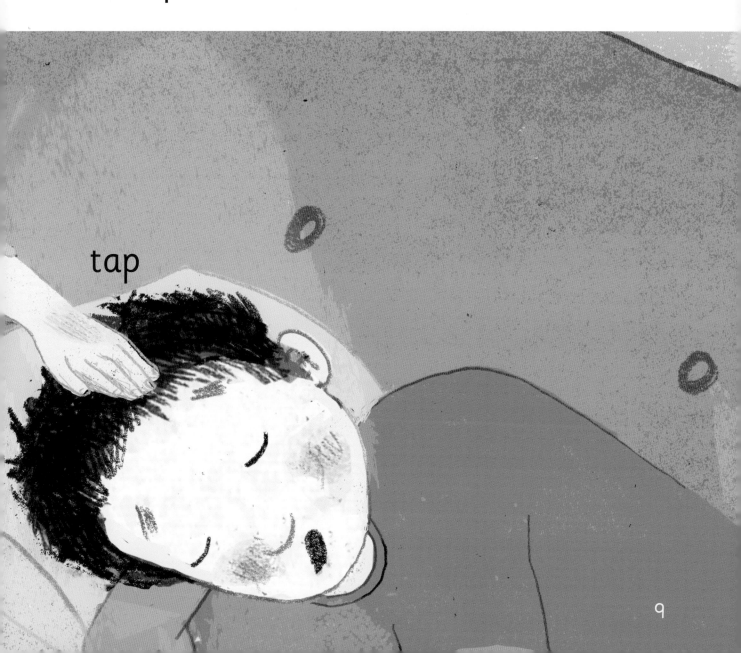

tap

Dad sits.

sip sip

pat pat
pat pat

11

pit pat pit pat

12

Dad dips in it!

14

After reading

Letters and Sounds: Phase 2

Word count: 44

Focus phonemes: /s/ /a/ /t/ /p/ /i/ /n/ /m/ /d/

Curriculum links: Understanding the world; Personal, social and emotional development

Early learning goals: Reading: read and understand simple sentences; use phonic knowledge to decode regular words and read them aloud accurately

Developing fluency

- Your child may enjoy hearing you read the book.
- Take turns to read a page with you beginning on page 2 to demonstrate how to read the sound words (**pit pat**) expressively. Check your child reads the words in the pictures too.
- Encourage your child to read the sentence with the exclamation mark (page 13) with a surprised or excited tone.

Phonic practice

- Point at **pads** on page 7 and ask your child to sound it out (p/a/d/s) and then blend.
- Turn to page 13. How many words can they find which contain the /d/ sound? Ask them to sound out and blend **Dad** and **dips**.
- Look at the "I spy sounds" pages (14–15). Point to the umbrella and say: I spy an /m/ – **umbrella**, emphasising the /m/ sound. Ask your child to find more things that contain the /m/ sound. (*Tim, mat, mirror, motorbike, jumper, mug, magazine, milk bottles, mud*)

Extending vocabulary

- On page 4, discuss how Tim is feeling (**sad**). Discuss other words that could describe how he feels. (e.g. *unhappy, miserable, down, fed up, bored*)
- On page 12, can your child think of words that describe how Tim is feeling now? (e.g. *happy, excited, cheerful, surprised*)